14 DAYS

AF534261

ATEEB DESHMUKH

Copyright © Ateeb Deshmukh
All Rights Reserved.

This book has been self-published with all reasonable efforts taken to make the material error-free by the author. No part of this book shall be used, reproduced in any manner whatsoever without written permission from the author, except in the case of brief quotations embodied in critical articles and reviews.

The Author of this book is solely responsible and liable for its content including but not limited to the views, representations, descriptions, statements, information, opinions and references ["Content"]. The Content of this book shall not constitute or be construed or deemed to reflect the opinion or expression of the Publisher or Editor. Neither the Publisher nor Editor endorse or approve the Content of this book or guarantee the reliability, accuracy or completeness of the Content published herein and do not make any representations or warranties of any kind, express or implied, including but not limited to the implied warranties of merchantability, fitness for a particular purpose. The Publisher and Editor shall not be liable whatsoever for any errors, omissions, whether such errors or omissions result from negligence, accident, or any other cause or claims for loss or damages of any kind, including without limitation, indirect or consequential loss or damage arising out of use, inability to use, or about the reliability, accuracy or sufficiency of the information contained in this book.

Made with ♥ on the Notion Press Platform
www.notionpress.com

Contents

Disclaimer

The book "14 Days" is a work of fiction and is not intended to be a guide to any real-life situations or events. The story contains elements of horror and suspense, and may not be suitable for all readers.

The plot revolves around a person who is challenged to live for 14 days until a demon kills him, and the events that unfold during this period. While the author has made efforts to ensure that the story is entertaining and engaging, the depiction of the demon and other supernatural elements is purely fictional.

The author does not condone or encourage any dangerous or life-threatening activities, and readers should not attempt to replicate any of the actions or events portrayed in the book.

The characters and events depicted in the book are entirely fictional and any resemblance to actual persons, living or dead, or to real events is purely coincidental.

Readers are advised to use their discretion before reading the book, and are solely responsible for any actions they take based on the information provided in the book. The author and publisher shall not be held responsible for any harm or loss resulting from the use of the information contained in the book.

CHAPTER ONE

The Demon's Curse

It started with a simple curiosity. Me and my friends stumbled upon a mysterious website promising to summon a demon. We did a dare between friends to see who could last the longest with the demon that haunted it. Being a skeptic, I thought it was all just a hoax. I didn't expect anything to happen when I followed the instructions.

But I was wrong.

After reciting the incantation, I felt a sudden chill in the air. The room grew dark, and a gust of wind knocked me off my feet. When I opened my eyes, I saw a pair of glowing red orbs staring at me.

"You have summoned me, mortal," a raspy voice echoed in my mind. "What is your wish?"

I froze in fear, realizing the gravity of my mistake. I didn't want to make a wish or deal with a demon. I just wanted to prove that the website was a scam. But it was too late.

"I... I don't want anything," I stammered. "Please go back to where you came from."

The demon chuckled, a sound that made my blood run cold. "I'm afraid I can't do that. You have invoked my presence, and now you must pay the price."

"What price?" I asked, trying to buy time.

"The curse of the demon," it replied. "You have fourteen days to live. And every day, you will face a challenge that will test your will and strength. Fail, and you will die. Succeed, and you will buy yourself some time. But eventually, your fate is sealed."

I couldn't believe what I was hearing. A curse? Challenges? Death? It sounded like a bad horror movie plot. But the demon's eyes gleamed with malice, and I knew it was real.

"Please, there must be a way to break the curse," I pleaded.

The demon shrugged. "Maybe. But you'll have to figure it out yourself. Good luck, mortal. You'll need it."

And with that, the demon vanished, leaving me alone in the dark. I sat there, shivering with fear and uncertainty. What have I done? How could I get out of this mess? I had no idea. All I knew was that I was in for the ride of my life, and it wasn't going to be a pleasant one.

CHAPTER TWO

THE DEMON'S CHALLENGE

As soon as I woke up on the second day after summoning the demon, I knew something was wrong. My body felt heavy and sluggish, and my head was pounding with a migraine. I tried to get up from the bed, but my legs gave out beneath me, and I fell back down, groaning in pain.

"What the hell is going on?" I muttered to myself, my voice raspy and weak.

As I lay there, trying to catch my breath, I suddenly heard a voice in my head. It was a low, menacing growl, like the sound of a wild animal about to attack.

"Good morning, mortal," the demon's voice said. "I trust you slept well?"

I gritted my teeth, trying to ignore the pain and fear that was flooding my mind. "What do you want?" I demanded, my voice shaking with anger and terror.

The demon chuckled, and I could feel its presence looming over me like a dark cloud. "Oh, nothing much. Just wanted to give you a little challenge for today."

I braced myself for whatever was coming, knowing that I had no choice but to face it head-on.

"What kind of challenge?" I asked, my voice barely above a whisper.

The demon's voice grew even colder and more menacing. "I want you to confront your deepest fears. The things that keep you up at night, the nightmares that haunt your dreams. Face them head-on, or suffer the consequences."

With that, the voice disappeared, leaving me alone in the darkness of my own thoughts.

I knew what the demon was asking of me, and I knew it was going to be the hardest thing I had ever done. But I also knew that I had no other choice if I wanted to survive.

Taking a deep breath, I closed my eyes and let the memories come flooding back.

I saw the faces of all the people I had lost in my life - my parents, my sister, my best friend. I felt the weight of my own failures and shortcomings, the mistakes I had made that had led me down this dark path.

But then, something shifted inside me. I realized that I couldn't keep running from these fears, that I had to face them head-on and conquer them if I wanted to be free.

And so, with a newfound sense of determination, I got up from the bed and faced the day ahead, ready for whatever challenges lay ahead.

CHAPTER THREE

The Haunting Begins

As soon as I woke up on the third day, I knew something was wrong. The air in my room was thick and heavy, and I could hear faint whispers coming from every corner of the room. I sat up in my bed, my heart racing, and tried to shake off the feeling of dread that was slowly creeping over me.

I got out of bed and walked around my room, trying to find the source of the whispers. But no matter how hard I tried, I couldn't pinpoint where they were coming from. They seemed to be everywhere and nowhere at the same time.

I tried to ignore them and went about my day as usual, but the feeling of unease never left me. As the day progressed, the whispers grew louder and more intense, until they were almost unbearable. I could hear them even when I was outside, and I knew that I was being followed.

That night, as I lay in bed, I could feel something watching me. I tried to ignore it and closed my eyes, hoping to fall asleep, but the feeling only grew stronger. And then, suddenly, I felt something touch me.

It was a cold, bony hand, and it gripped my arm tightly. I opened my eyes, but I couldn't see anything. The room was shrouded in darkness, and the only sound was the faint whispering that seemed to be coming from right next to me.

I tried to pull away, but the hand held on tightly, and I could feel something pulling me towards the foot of the bed. I was paralyzed with fear, and I couldn't move or scream.

And then, just as suddenly as it had started, it stopped. The hand released its grip, and the whispers faded away. I was left alone in the darkness, my heart pounding in my chest.

I knew then that I was not alone in my house. The demon had arrived, and it was determined to kill me.

CHAPTER FOUR

The Possessed Doll

I woke up to find myself still alive. But the relief was short-lived. As I tried to get out of bed, I heard a soft laughter coming from the corner of the room. I looked over and saw an old porcelain doll sitting on a shelf. I didn't remember bringing it here, but maybe it was just one of those things that you don't remember doing.

The laughter grew louder, and I could feel a chill run down my spine. I tried to ignore it and went to take a shower. But as soon as I opened the bathroom door, I saw the doll sitting on the toilet seat. Its eyes were black, and its smile was twisted. I froze in fear, unable to move.

The doll suddenly jumped off the seat and landed on the floor. It started to move towards me, its limbs contorting in unnatural ways. I backed away, but it was like it was following me. It was like it was possessed.

I knew what I had to do. I grabbed a towel and threw it over the doll, hoping to smother it. But it was stronger than I thought. It broke free and started to crawl towards me. I could see its black eyes staring into mine, and I felt like I was going to lose my mind.

I ran out of the bathroom and into the living room. I tried to calm myself down, but then I heard the doll laughing again. I turned around, and there it was, sitting on the couch, staring at me.

I knew what I had to do. I grabbed a lighter and a can of hairspray and started to douse the doll with it. I knew it was risky, but I had no choice. I lit a match and threw it at the doll, watching it burst into flames.

I felt a sense of relief wash over me as I watched the doll burn. But then I heard the demon's voice in my head. "You can't escape me, mortal. You can't run from your fate."

I knew the demon was right. I had only 10 days left to live, and I had no idea what else it had in store for me. I knew I had to be prepared for anything. I just didn't know how.

CHAPTER FIVE

The Unsettling Presence

I woke up with a jolt, my heart racing as if it was about to burst out of my chest. It was day 5, and I knew I had to prepare myself for whatever challenge the demon had in store for me today.

As I got out of bed, I felt an unsettling presence in the room. It was as if someone was watching me, even though I knew I was alone. I shuddered and tried to shake off the feeling, but it lingered like a bad omen.

I decided to take a shower, hoping that the warm water would calm my nerves. But as I stood under the spray, I couldn't shake off the feeling that I was being watched. I quickly washed up and got out of the shower, wrapping a towel around myself.

As I walked back to my bedroom, I noticed that some of the pictures on the walls were askew. I couldn't remember if I had left them like that or if the demon had tampered with them. I straightened them out, but the feeling of unease lingered.

I decided to make breakfast, hoping that some food would settle my nerves. But as I stood in the kitchen, I noticed that some of the dishes were missing. I searched the cupboards and drawers, but I couldn't find them anywhere. It was as if they had vanished into thin air.

I tried to brush it off and made some eggs and toast. But as I ate, I noticed that my food tasted off. It was as if there was something wrong with it, something that I couldn't quite put my finger on.

The rest of the day passed in a blur of unease and uncertainty. Every time I turned around, it felt like something was watching me. I heard strange noises in the walls, and I could swear that I saw shadows moving in the corners of my eyes.

As the day drew to a close, I realized that the demon had won. It had managed to get inside my head, to make me doubt my own senses. I was trapped in a world of fear and paranoia, and I knew that I couldn't escape it.

I went to bed that night, knowing that the demon would be back the next day. And as I closed my eyes, I couldn't shake off the feeling that I was being watched.

CHAPTER SIX

The Betrayal

As the sun rose on the sixth day, I found myself in a state of confusion and fear. The events of the previous day had left me drained and terrified, and I was beginning to wonder if there was any way to beat this demon and survive.

As I stumbled out of bed, my mind raced with thoughts of what the demon might have in store for me today. Would it be another physical challenge, like the one I had faced on day two? Or would it be something more insidious, like the mental torment of day four?

As I made my way to the bathroom, I caught sight of myself in the mirror and was shocked at what I saw. My once-vibrant complexion was now sallow and pale, and there were dark circles under my eyes. I knew that I was running out of time, and that I had to find a way to break the curse before it was too late.

With a sense of determination, I headed downstairs to face whatever challenge awaited me. But as I stepped into the living room, I was met with a sight that made my blood run cold.

Standing in the center of the room was my best friend, Sarah. But something was different about her. Her eyes were black as coal, and a malevolent grin spread across her face as she approached me.

"Hello, dear friend," she hissed. "I've come to deliver a message from our friend down below."

My heart sank as I realized that Sarah had been possessed by the demon. I had trusted her with my life, and now she was working against me.

"What do you want?" I demanded, trying to keep my voice steady.

"I want you to know that there's no way out of this," Sarah said. "The demon has already won. And in case you were wondering, today's challenge is simple. You just have to survive the day."

With that, she turned and walked out of the room, leaving me alone with my thoughts. I knew that I had to find a way to break the curse, but I had no idea where to begin.

As the day wore on, I felt my anxiety mounting. Every sound made me jump; every shadow seemed to hold a lurking danger. And as the hours passed, I began to realize that Sarah wasn't the only one working against me.

Throughout the day, I caught glimpses of people I knew, all of them wearing the same black-eyed expression that Sarah had. It was as if the demon had taken over the entire town, turning everyone I knew and loved into his pawns.

As the sun began to set, I retreated to my bedroom, locking the door behind me. But even here, I wasn't safe. The walls seemed to be closing in on me, and I could feel the demon's presence growing stronger with each passing moment.

In the end, I knew that I was no match for the demon's power. As the clock struck midnight, I felt a cold hand wrap around my throat, and I knew that my time had run out.

With a final gasp, I succumbed to the demon's curse, knowing that I had lost the battle. But even as the darkness overtook me, I held onto a small glimmer of hope. I knew that one day, someone would come along who would be brave enough to face the demon and break his curse once and for all. And in that moment, I knew that my sacrifice had not been in vain.

CHAPTER SEVEN

The Fear of Darkness

The sixth day had come and gone, and I was still alive. However, the fear of the unknown was starting to take its toll on me. Every creak and rustle in the darkened corners of my apartment made me jump. I was afraid to close my eyes, fearing that when I opened them, the demon would be there waiting for me.

I knew that I needed to find a way to conquer my fear, or else I would never make it to the end of the fourteen days. So, I decided to face it head-on. I turned off all the lights in my apartment and sat in the darkness, forcing myself to confront my fears.

At first, I could barely breathe. The darkness was suffocating, and I could feel my heart racing. But slowly, I began to calm down. I realized that the darkness was just an absence of light, and that nothing was going to harm me if I couldn't see it.

As I sat there, I started to notice things that I hadn't before. The faint glow of the moonlight shining through my window, the hum of the refrigerator in the kitchen, and the distant sound of a car driving down the street. I realized that even in the darkness, there was still life around me.

After a few hours, I turned the lights back on, feeling victorious. I had faced my fear and come out on the other side. However, my victory was short-lived. As I sat on my couch, I heard a soft whisper in my ear, "You can't escape me."

I whipped my head around, but there was no one there. The demon had found a way to get inside my head. And it was only a matter of time before it found a way to get to me.

CHAPTER EIGHT

THE HUNT

I woke up early on the eighth day, feeling more refreshed than I had in days. I knew what I had to do today, and I was ready for it. I grabbed my laptop and headed to the coffee shop down the street, hoping to find some answers.

I spent hours poring over books, websites, and forums, trying to find any information I could about the demon that was coming for me. I was starting to feel like I was never going to find anything useful when I stumbled upon an old blog post from a woman who claimed to have encountered the same demon years ago.

According to her, the demon was known as the Hunter. It was relentless, and it wouldn't stop until it had claimed its victim. But there was one weakness that the Hunter had - it could only see in black and white.

I was skeptical at first, but the more I read, the more convinced I became that this was my only chance to survive. I had to figure out a way to use this weakness against the demon.

I spent the rest of the day searching for anything that could help me, and eventually, I found a small shop that sold special glasses that could filter out colors. I bought a pair and headed back to my apartment to get some rest before the next half of the day's challenge.

The next half of the day was filled with tension as I prepared for my showdown with the Hunter. I put on my glasses and headed out to face my enemy.

The streets were eerily quiet as I walked, my heart racing with fear and anticipation. I knew that the Hunter could be lurking around any corner, waiting to strike.

I turned a corner and saw it - the demon was standing in the middle of the street, its eyes fixed on me. I could feel its malevolent energy emanating from its dark form, and I knew that this was it. This was the moment of truth.

I took a deep breath and stepped forward; my eyes locked on the demon. It was a strange sensation, looking at the world in black and white. Everything was so stark and surreal.

The Hunter began to move toward me, its movements slow and deliberate. I could see the veins in its wings pulsing with dark energy, and I knew that I had to act quickly.

I raised my hand and focused all of my energy on the demon. I could feel a surge of power coursing through me, and I channeled it into a beam of pure light.

The beam struck the Hunter, and it let out a terrible scream as it disintegrated into nothingness. I stood there for a moment, catching my breath, and then I removed my glasses.

The world was back to normal, and I felt a sense of relief wash over me. I had survived another day, and I was one step closer to defeating the demon once and for all. But I knew that there were still many challenges ahead, and I had to stay strong if I was going to make it to the end.

CHAPTER NINE

A Visitor from Beyond

I woke up feeling restless and uneasy. I had a nightmare that a grotesque creature was hovering over me, its long sharp claws ready to tear me apart. It was the same demon that had been haunting me for the past few days. I quickly shook off the feeling and reminded myself that it was just a bad dream.

But as I got out of bed, I noticed something strange. My room was freezing cold, despite the fact that it was the middle of summer. The air felt heavy and thick, as if something was weighing it down. I looked around and saw a strange shadow in the corner of the room. It was the same shape as the demon that had been following me.

I stood frozen, unable to move or speak. The shadow began to move, growing larger and larger until it filled the entire room. I could hear its deep breathing, as if it was enjoying the fear that it was causing me.

Suddenly, the shadow dissipated, and in its place stood a woman. She was tall and thin, with pale skin and jet-black hair that hung in loose curls around her shoulders. She wore a long, flowing gown that seemed to shimmer in the dim light.

"Who are you?" I asked, my voice shaking with fear.

"I am Lilith," she replied, her voice soft and musical. "I have been sent by the demon to deliver a message to you."

"What message?" I asked, still trembling.

"The demon wants you to know that it is coming for you," Lilith said. "You have only five days left, and then it will be too late."

I felt a lump form in my throat. I had known that the demon would come for me eventually, but I had hoped that I would have more time to prepare.

"What can I do?" I asked.

"Nothing," Lilith said. "The demon has already set its sights on you. You can't run, you can't hide. It will find you no matter where you go."

I felt a surge of anger and frustration. I refused to let this demon control my life. I would fight back, no matter what.

"Thank you for the warning," I said, my voice steady. "But I won't give up without a fight."

Lilith smiled. "That's the spirit," she said. "But be careful. The demon is powerful, and it will stop at nothing to destroy you."

With that, Lilith vanished into thin air, leaving me alone in the cold, dark room.

I knew that I had to come up with a plan. I couldn't just sit around and wait for the demon to come for me. I needed to be proactive, to take control of the situation.

But as I sat down to brainstorm ideas, I couldn't help but feel a sense of dread. The demon was coming for me, and there was nothing I could do to stop it.

I had four days left. Four days to come up with a plan, to fight back against the demon. Four days to save my own life.

CHAPTER TEN

THE HAUNTED HOUSE

I woke up on the tenth day with a sense of dread in my stomach. I knew that the challenge for the day would be one of the toughest yet. I had heard rumors of a haunted house on the outskirts of town, and I had a feeling that this was where I would have to go.

I got dressed quickly and headed out, trying to mentally prepare myself for what was to come. As I approached the house, I could feel my heart racing in my chest. The house looked like something straight out of a horror movie, with creaky shutters and a front door that looked like it hadn't been opened in years.

I took a deep breath and pushed the door open, stepping into the darkness of the house. The air was thick with the smell of dust and mildew, and I could hear strange noises coming from every corner.

I walked cautiously through the house, my heart pounding in my chest with every step. As I turned a corner, I saw a figure standing in the hallway ahead of me. It was a woman, dressed in old-fashioned clothes, and she was staring at me with empty eyes.

I tried to turn and run, but something seemed to be holding me back. I was paralyzed with fear, unable to move as the woman stepped closer and closer.

Suddenly, she lunged at me, and I felt something cold and sharp pierce my skin. I screamed in agony as the demon's curse took hold, knowing that I only had a few more days left to live.

CHAPTER ELEVEN

THE LOST SOUL

I woke up in a strange place, unsure of how I got there. The room was dark, and I couldn't see anything except for a faint glow coming from a corner of the room. As my eyes adjusted to the darkness, I realized that the glow was coming from a small lantern.

I got up and walked towards the lantern, and as I got closer, I saw that there was a note attached to it. It read, "Find the lost soul and bring it back to the light."

I had no idea what this meant, but I knew that I had to find the lost soul. I searched the room, but there was no one else there. I walked out of the room and found myself in a dark hallway. The only light came from the lantern that I was carrying.

I started to walk down the hallway, unsure of where I was going or what I was looking for. I turned a corner, and suddenly, I heard a sound. It was a faint whisper, and it seemed to be coming from the end of the hallway.

I walked towards the source of the sound, and as I got closer, I realized that it was a voice. It was a woman's voice, and she was calling out for help.

"Please, help me," she said. "I'm lost, and I can't find my way back to the light."

I followed the sound of her voice, and soon, I found myself in a room. In the center of the room was a woman. She was sitting on the ground, and she looked terrified.

"Who are you?" I asked.

"I'm the lost soul," she said. "I've been trapped here for so long, and I don't know how to get back to the light."

I didn't know what to do, but I knew that I had to help her. I reached out my hand to her, and she took it. We stood up, and I led her out of the room and back into the hallway.

As we walked, the hallway started to get brighter, and soon, we were surrounded by light. We emerged from the hallway and found ourselves in a beautiful garden.

The woman looked around, and she smiled. "Thank you," she said. "You saved me."

I was relieved that I had completed the challenge, but I couldn't shake the feeling that something was wrong. I knew that I only had a few days left, and I still had no idea how to defeat the demon.

I looked around the garden, searching for any clues, and that's when I saw it. In the center of the garden was a statue of a demon. It was the same demon that had been haunting me for the past few days.

I approached the statue, and as I got closer, I saw that there was another note attached to it. It read, "You cannot defeat the demon alone. You will need help."

I didn't know who could help me, but I knew that I had to find someone. I left the garden, determined to find a way to defeat the demon before it was too late.

CHAPTER TWELVE

THE HAUNTED HOTEL

As soon as I woke up on Day 12, I felt a sense of dread wash over me. The challenge for the day was to spend a night in a haunted hotel. I couldn't even begin to imagine the horrors that awaited me.

I packed a bag with a change of clothes, a flashlight, and some snacks, trying to push the anxiety out of my mind. I didn't want to dwell on what might happen. I just wanted to get it over with.

When I arrived at the hotel, it was clear that it had seen better days. The paint was peeling, the windows were broken, and the doors creaked ominously. I took a deep breath and stepped inside, determined to complete the challenge.

The lobby was dark and deserted, and I had to use my flashlight to navigate. I checked in at the front desk and was given a key to room 666. As I made my way to the elevator, I couldn't shake the feeling that I was being watched.

When I arrived at my room, I hesitated for a moment before unlocking the door. I pushed it open slowly, and was greeted by a cold draft and the sound of creaking floorboards. The room was sparsely furnished, with a single bed, a dresser, and a mirror that was covered in grime.

I sat down on the bed and tried to relax, but my mind was racing. I kept imagining that I could hear whispers and footsteps, even though the room was completely still. I decided to explore the hotel and see if there was anyone else around.

As I walked down the hallway, I noticed that the doors to the other rooms were open. I peered inside a few of them, but they were all empty. The hotel was completely deserted, except for me.

I continued down the hallway until I reached a staircase. I descended into the basement, where I found a room that was filled with old furniture and cobwebs. It looked like it hadn't been touched in years.

Suddenly, I heard a noise behind me. I turned around to see a figure standing in the shadows. It was difficult to make out any features, but I could tell that it was tall and thin. I was frozen with fear.

The figure began to move towards me, and I could hear its footsteps echoing through the basement. I tried to run, but my legs felt like they were made of lead. I stumbled and fell, and the figure was upon me.

I screamed as it reached out and touched me, but then everything went black.

When I woke up, I was back in my own bed. The clock read 14 days exactly since the demon was launched back to me. I had failed the challenge, and now I was out of time. The demon had come for me, and there was nothing I could do to stop it.

CHAPTER THIRTEEN

The Final Countdown

I woke up early on day 13, feeling more exhausted than ever. My eyes were heavy, and my body felt numb. It was like all the energy had been drained out of me. I tried to get up from my bed, but my legs refused to cooperate. They felt weak and shaky, and I stumbled a couple of times before I finally managed to stand on my feet.

I knew something was wrong with me. I couldn't explain it, but I felt like I was slowly fading away, like a candle flickering in the wind. And then, I heard a whisper, a voice that seemed to be coming from inside my head.

"Your time is running out, mortal," the demon's voice hissed. "You have only one day left, and then, you will be mine forever."

I shuddered at the thought of spending an eternity in hell. But then, I realized something. I had faced all the challenges the demon had thrown at me, and I had survived them all. I had proven to myself that I was stronger than I ever thought I was.

With that realization, a surge of energy coursed through my veins. I felt a renewed sense of purpose, and I knew what I had to do. I had to confront the demon once and for all.

I got dressed and left my apartment. The sky was cloudy, and the air was heavy with a sense of foreboding. I walked to the abandoned church where I had first summoned the demon, and I saw it waiting for me, its eyes glowing with a fierce intensity.

"You cannot defeat me," it snarled. "I am beyond your puny mortal strength."

But I wasn't alone. I had brought with me a silver dagger that I had borrowed from a friend. It was an ancient weapon that had been blessed by a priest, and it had the power to vanquish evil.

I charged at the demon, my heart pounding with a mixture of fear and determination. The demon lunged at me, its claws flashing in the dim light. I dodged its attack and stabbed it with the silver dagger.

The demon shrieked in agony as its body dissolved into a cloud of smoke. I felt a sense of triumph, but then, something strange happened. The smoke coalesced into a humanoid figure, and I recognized it as the demon's true form.

"You have defeated me, mortal," the demon said, its voice weak and raspy. "But you have also sealed your own fate. You have broken the pact, and now, you will suffer the consequences."

And then, the demon vanished into thin air, leaving me alone in the abandoned church. I felt a chill run down my spine as I realized what the demon had meant. I had broken the pact, and that meant that I had only 24 hours left to live.

I stumbled out of the church, my mind reeling with fear and confusion. I didn't know what to do or where to go. But then, I remembered something. There was one person who could help me, one person who had always been there for me, no matter what.

I ran to my best friend's house, hoping against hope that he would believe me and help me. I told him everything, from the day I had summoned the demon to the moment I had killed it. He listened intently, his eyes wide with disbelief.

"I believe you," he said finally. "And I will do everything in my power to help you."

We spent the rest of the day researching ways to break a demon's curse. We consulted books, searched the internet, and even visited a local psychic. But nothing seemed to work. The curse was too powerful, and time was running.

CHAPTER FOURTEEN

The End

As I woke up on the fourteenth day, I knew it was the end. I had failed the challenge, and now the demon was coming to take my soul.

I could feel its presence in the room, the air thick with the stench of sulfur and brimstone. I had tried everything to escape my fate, but there was no way out. I had run, I had hidden, I had even tried to fight, but it was all in vain.

As I sat in the corner of the room, trembling with fear, the demon appeared before me. Its eyes were blazing with a fiery red, and its skin was black as coal. It towered over me, its massive wings unfurled as it reached out to grab me.

I closed my eyes and waited for the end, but it didn't come. Instead, I felt a cold, hard grip on my shoulder, and a voice whispered in my ear.

"Come with me," it said. "I will take you away from here."

I opened my eyes to see a figure standing before me, clad in a long black robe with a hood covering its face. I couldn't see who or what it was, but I knew it wasn't human.

I hesitated for a moment, unsure whether to trust this stranger or not, but then I remembered the demon and decided to take my chances.

I got up and followed the figure out of the room and into a long, dark hallway. We walked for what felt like hours, passing by countless doors and corridors, until we finally came to a large, ornate gate.

The figure produced a key and unlocked the gate, pushing it open to reveal a blinding light. I shielded my eyes and stepped through, and when I opened them again, I found myself in a beautiful garden.

The sun was shining, and the air was filled with the scent of flowers. Birds chirped and butterflies fluttered around me, and I felt a sense of peace and tranquility wash over me.

I turned to thank the figure for saving me, but it was gone. I looked around, but there was no sign of it. I was alone in the garden, and I knew that I had been given a second chance.

I spent the rest of my days in that garden, enjoying its beauty and serenity. I never forgot about the demon, but I knew that it could never touch me again.

And so I lived the rest of my life in peace, grateful for the stranger who had saved me from a fate worse than death. I knew that I had been given a second chance, and I was determined to make the most of it.

CHAPTER FIFTEEN

THE REALITY

As I sit in my hospital bed, the reality of my situation sinks in. The demon that I had been battling for the past two weeks was not a supernatural being, but rather a disease that had been slowly consuming my body for months.

The doctors had told me that I had cancer, and that it had spread too far for any treatment to be effective. They had given me 14 days to live.

At first, I was in denial. I couldn't believe that the demon that had haunted me for the past two weeks was actually the physical manifestation of my own mortality.

But as the days went by, I began to accept my fate. I knew that I had to make peace with myself and with those around me before it was too late.

I started writing letters to my loved ones, telling them how much they meant to me and how grateful I was to have them in my life. I made amends with people I had hurt in the past and forgave those who had wronged me.

I also reflected on the challenges that I had faced during the past two weeks. Each day had been a test of my strength and resilience, but it had also taught me valuable lessons about life and death.

I realized that the demon had not been sent to punish me, but rather to teach me the importance of living every day to the fullest and cherishing the people and moments that matter most.

As I write these final words, I know that my time is running out. But I also know that I am leaving behind a legacy of love and forgiveness that will live on long after I am gone.

So to anyone who may be reading this, I urge you to take each day as a gift and to never take your loved ones for granted. Life is precious, and it can be taken away at any moment.

May my story serve as a reminder to cherish every moment, to love deeply, and to never give up hope.

Printed by Libri Plureos GmbH in Hamburg,
Germany